For Ted, who would have been pleased
—L. M.

For Natsuko
—P. P.-R.

G. P. Putnam's Sons
a division of Penguin Putnam Books for Young Readers,
345 Hudson Street, New York, NY 10014.
G. P. Putnam's Sons, Reg. U.S. Pat. & Tm. Off.
Published simultaneously in Canada.
Manufactured in China by South China Printing Co. Ltd.
Book designed by Gina DiMassi.
Text set in Sister Medium.
The art was done in gouache.
Library of Congress Cataloging-in-Publication Data
Moss, Lloyd. Music is / written by Lloyd Moss ; illustrations by Philippe Petit-Roulet.
p. cm.   Summary: A rhyming salute to the many ways in which people enjoy music.
[1. Music—Fiction. 2. Stories in rhyme.] I. Petit-Roulet, Philippe, ill. II. Title.
PZ8.3.M8464 Mu 2003   [E]—dc21   00-067328
ISBN 0-399-23336-9
1 3 5 7 9 10 8 6 4 2
First Impression

Music Is

written by
Lloyd Moss

illustrations by
Philippe Petit-Roulet

G. P. Putnam's Sons
New York

music fills our lives with magic;
music is a wondrous thing.
Music bright or music tragic,
music makes you cry or sing.

In the morning when you wake up,
nighttime when you go to bed,
music's always there to take up
lots of space inside your head.

Music makes my **foot start tapping**. Music makes me wave my hand.

Singing, humming, chanting, rapping; fingers snapping.

Music's grand!

Music is a magic potion. Happy music makes me smile.

Music's like a mighty ocean, full of motion all the while.

Music plays when people marry,
music when your birthday's here.
Just before it's January,
on the last day of the year.

Music when we go parading on the 4th day of July.

Music after **daylig**ht's fading; serenading lullaby.

Music
in
the
elevator,

sometimes music
on the phone.

After school or on a date or

later when
I'm all alone.

Music when a band is coming,
sounding out a

MARCHING
SONG.

Bugles blare

to sounds of drumming, and I'm humming right along.

Symphony or horn concerto,
  I compare to **heaven's sound.**
Any orchestras that care to
  sure can play while I'm around.

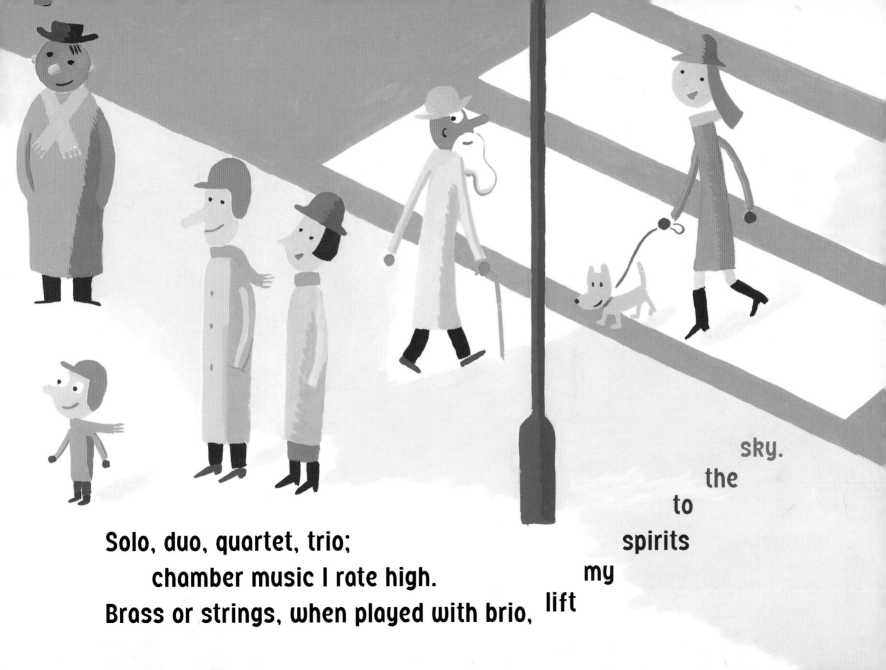

Solo, duo, quartet, trio;
    chamber music I rate high.
Brass or strings, when played with brio, lift my spirits to the sky.

Sondheim,   Bach or Ellington;
        Rodgers,   Mozart,
        Gershwin,   Porter,

any time,
   in any order,
      all their music's lots of fun.

Verdi, Humperdinck, Puccini;
opera is such a thrill.
Those by Bizet and Rossini please me,
and they always will.

TANGO,
rumba,
cha-cha,
mambo,
music with a hip-hop beat.
Any number, any combo, gets me up and on my feet.

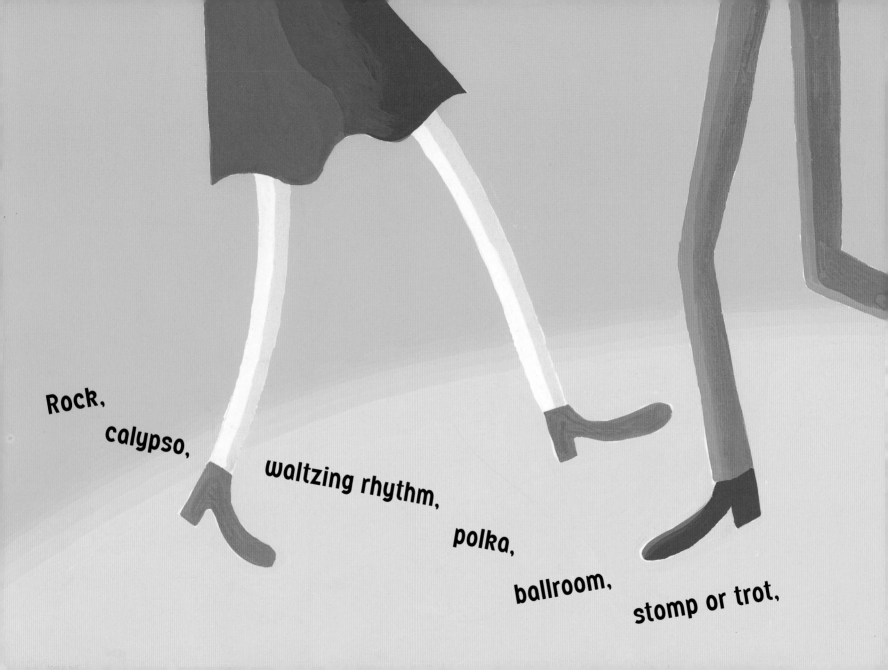

Rock, calypso, waltzing rhythm, polka, ballroom, stomp or trot,

it's a trip,

so I dance with them.

Large room, small room, matters not.

Music has an eerie power;
    music is my truest friend,
        brightening a lonely hour,
           comforting from start to end.

If there never had been music,
   if it never did exist,
      what would life be without music?
         Think of what we would have missed!

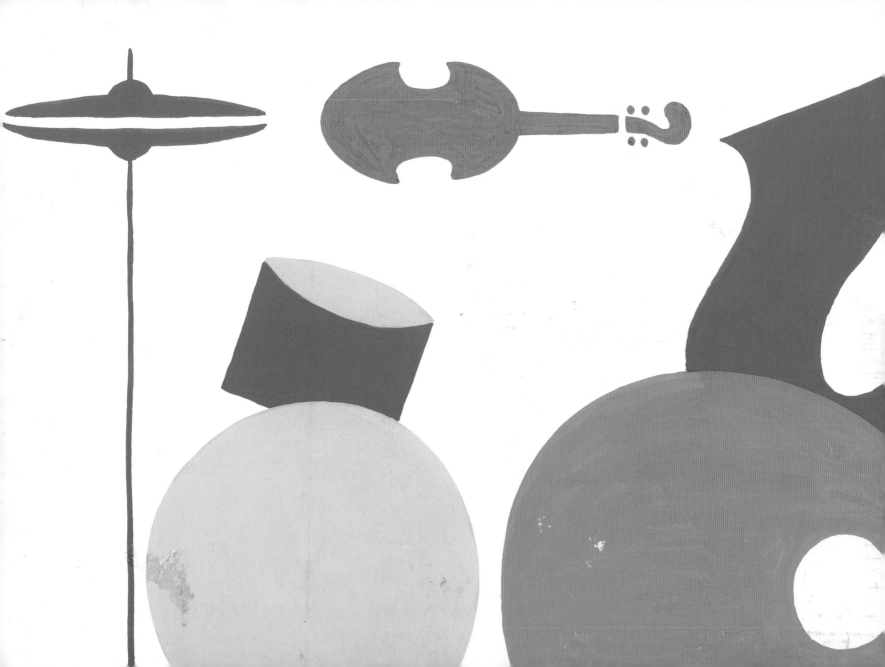